When picture book masters
Martin Waddell and Patrick Benson came
together to tell the story of three baby owls home alone,
they touched on a timeless truth – capturing the attachment
and deep affection between a mother and child with
humour and tenderness. A quarter of a century on, and over
four and a half million copies later, this perfectly crafted,
beautifully rendered story continues to comfort
young readers the world over.

For Hannah,
all-by-herself
M.W.

For Georgie,
and Eddie Huntley
P.B.

First published 1992 by Walker Books Ltd
87 Vauxhall Walk, London SE11 5HJ

This edition published 2017

10 9 8 7 6 5 4 3 2 1

Text © 1992 Martin Waddell

Illustrations © 1992 Patrick Benson

The right of Martin Waddell and Patrick Benson
to be identified as author and illustrator respectively
of this work has been asserted by them in accordance
with the Copyright, Designs and Patents Act 1988.

This book has been typeset in Caslon Antique

Printed in China

British Library Cataloguing in Publication Data:
a catalogue record for this book
is available from the British Library

ISBN 978-1-4063-4957-3

www.walker.co.uk

OWL BABIES

Written by
Martin Waddell

Illustrated by
Patrick Benson

WALKER BOOKS
AND SUBSIDIARIES
LONDON • BOSTON • SYDNEY • AUCKLAND

Once there were three baby owls:
Sarah and Percy and Bill.
They lived in a hole
in the trunk of a tree
with their Owl Mother.
The hole had twigs and
leaves and owl feathers in it.
It was their house.

One night they woke up and
their Owl Mother was GONE.

"Where's Mummy?" asked Sarah.

"Oh my goodness!" said Percy.

"I want my mummy!" said Bill.

The baby owls *thought*
(all owls think a lot) –
"I think she's gone hunting," said Sarah.
"To get us our food!" said Percy.
"I want my mummy!" said Bill.

But their Owl Mother didn't come.
The baby owls came out of
their house and they sat
on the tree and waited.

A big branch for Sarah,
a small branch for Percy,
and an old bit of ivy for Bill.
"She'll be back," said Sarah.
"Back *soon*!" said Percy.
"I want my mummy!" said Bill.

It was dark in the wood and
they had to be brave, for things
moved all around them.

"She'll bring us mice and
things that are nice," said Sarah.

"I suppose so!" said Percy.

"I want my mummy!" said Bill.

They sat and they thought
(all owls think a lot) –
"I think we should *all*
sit on *my* branch," said Sarah.
And they did,
all three together.

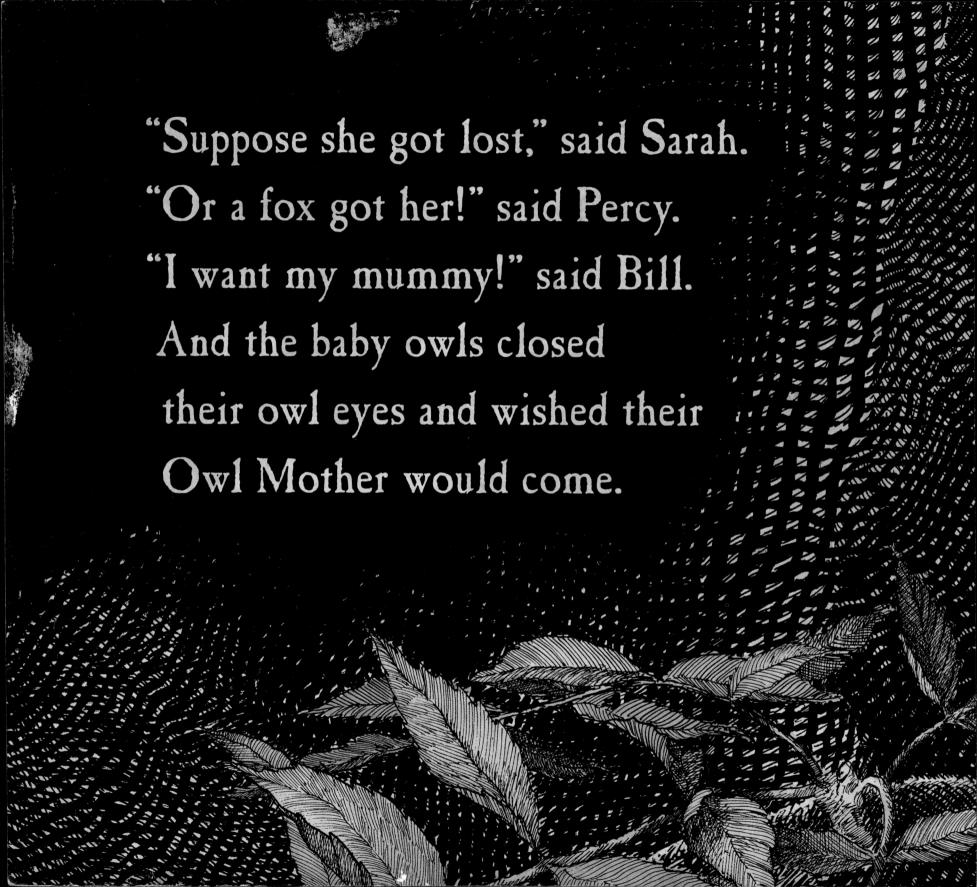

"Suppose she got lost," said Sarah.
"Or a fox got her!" said Percy.
"I want my mummy!" said Bill.
And the baby owls closed
their owl eyes and wished their
Owl Mother would come.

AND SHE CAME.

Soft and silent, she swooped
through the trees
to Sarah and Percy
and Bill.

"Mummy!" they cried,
and they flapped and they danced,
and they bounced up and down
on their branch.

"WHAT'S ALL THE FUSS?"
their Owl Mother asked.
"You knew I'd come back."
The baby owls thought
(all owls think a lot) –
"I knew it," said Sarah.
"And I knew it!" said Percy.
"I love my mummy!" said Bill.

This story came when I met a lost child
at a supermarket counter, eyes round with fear, repeating
again, and again, and again, "I want my mummy! I want my mummy!
I want my mummy!" Every child understands the fear behind those words
and the relief that comes with Patrick Benson's extraordinarily powerful
"AND SHE CAME" illustration. And I hope that every child can take away a
feeling of warmth and reassurance from *Owl Babies* – that they understand that
their fears are reasonable, and that the people who love them will always be
there for them. I love my owls ... particularly Bill. ~ *Martin Waddell*

The challenge for me, when illustrating Martin's wonderful words, was the need
to create a moonlit world which was realistically dark, but ultimately unthreatening.
I hope it's a world which helps children become less afraid of the night, and
a world which reassures children that, no matter how far away, Mum
will always be a comforting, protecting light in the darkness;
Mum will always come back home. ~ *Patrick Benson*